Mary had a little lamb

Mary had a little lamb,

Its fleece was white as snow,

And everywhere that Mary went,

The lamb was sure to go.

It followed her to school one day,

Which was against the rule,

It made the children laugh and play

To see a lamb at school.

And so the teacher turned it out,

But still it lingered near,

And waited patiently about

Till Mary did appear.

"Why does the lamb love Mary so?"

The eager children cry.

"Why, Mary loves the lamb, you know,"

The teacher did reply.

FOR ALFRED AND ELEANOR - KWC

First published in 2011 by Hodder Children's Books

Hodder Children's Books, 338 Euston Road, London, NW1 3BH
Hodder Children's Books Australia, Level 17/207 Kent Street, Sydney,
NSW 2000

A catalogue record of this book is available from the British Library.

ISBN 978 0 340 99977 6 (HB)
ISBN 978 0 340 99976 9 (PB)

10 9 8 7 6 5 4 3 2 1

Printed in China

Hodder Children's Books is a division of Hachette Children's Books,
an Hachette UK Company

www.hachette.co.uk

Mary had a little lamb

KATE WILLIS-CROWLEY

A division of Hachette Children's Books

Mary had a little lamb,
its fleece was white as snow,

And everywhere that Mary went,

the lamb was sure to go.

It followed her to school one day,
which was against the rule,

It made the children laugh and play

to see a lamb at school.

And so the teacher turned it out,

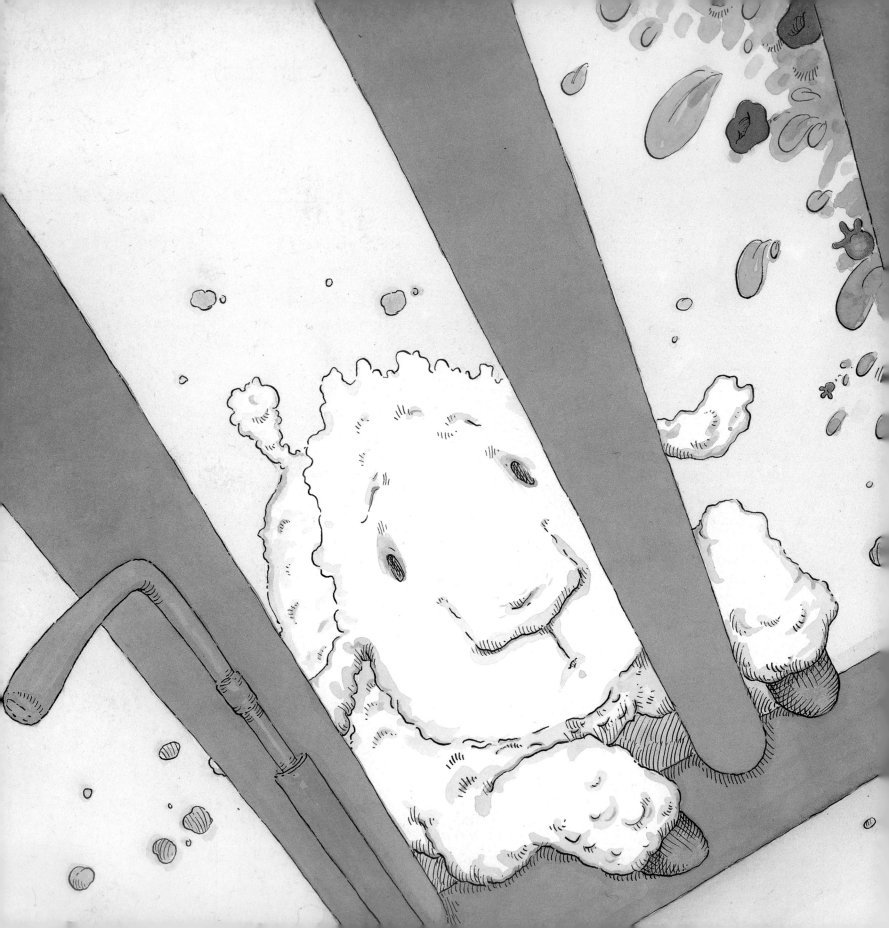

But still it lingered near,

And waited patiently about

till Mary did appear.

"Why does the lamb love Mary so?"
the eager children cry.

"Why, Mary loves the lamb, you know,"
the teacher did reply.

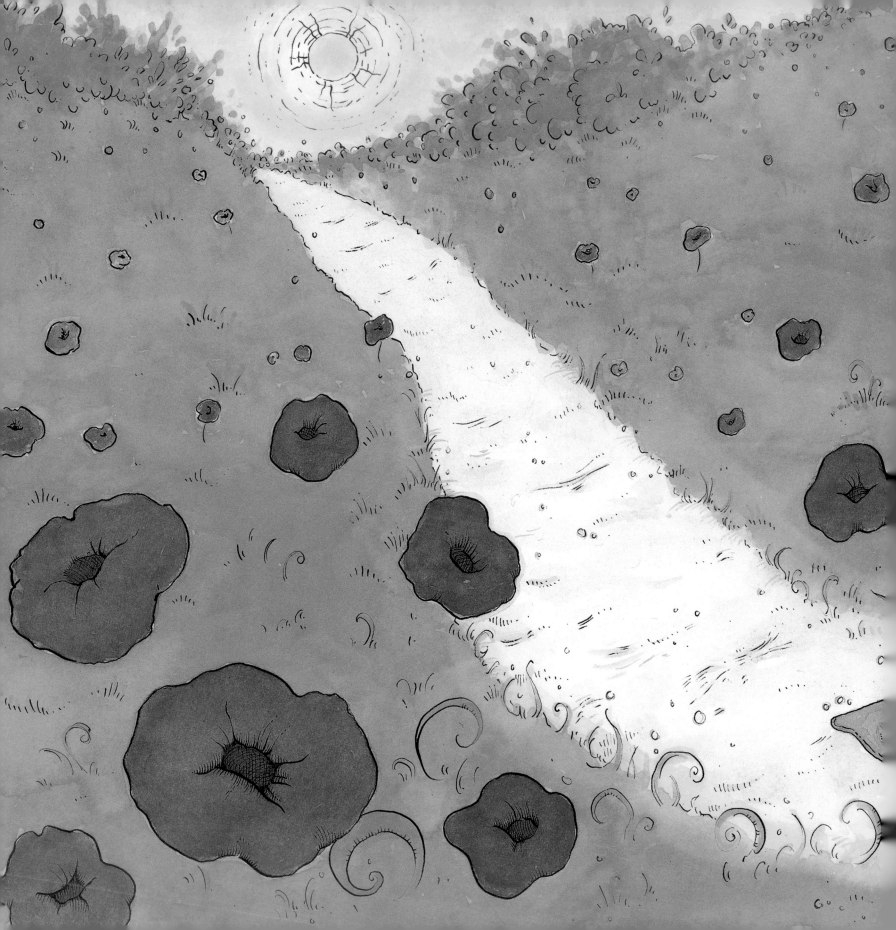

Make a 'Little Lamb' mask!

You need:

A grown-up to help, especially with cutting
A paper plate
Card
String
Cotton wool
Glue
Sticky tape
Scissors
Pens, pencils or crayons

1. With help, hold the paper plate up to your face and mark with a pencil where your eyes and nose are. Then, carefully cut out eye holes and a little hole for your nose.

2. Draw two long teardrop shapes on the card and carefully cut them out. These are the ears! Glue the ears to the back of the plate, so that they stick out, one on each side.

3. Decorate the mask with fluffy cotton wool and draw on the rest of the face.

4. Cut two long pieces of string and tape one above each ear, so that the mask can be tied on behind your head. Have fun, little lamb!

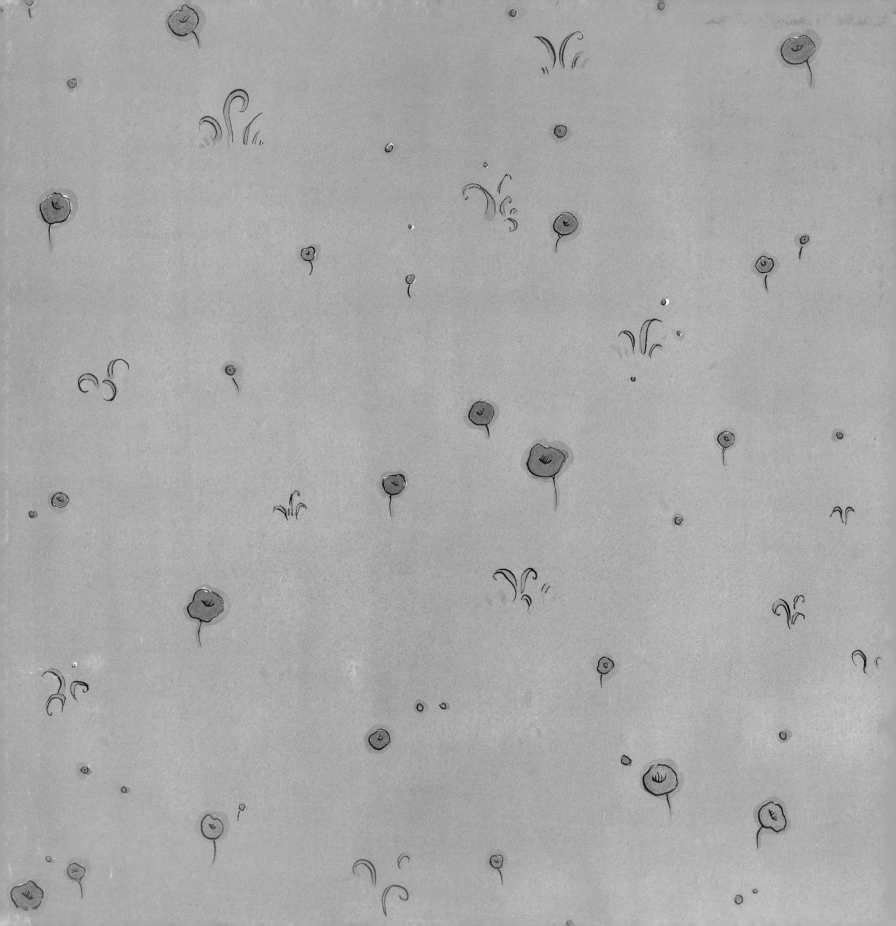